TIME MACHINE MAGAZINE

Sports Illustrated KIDS

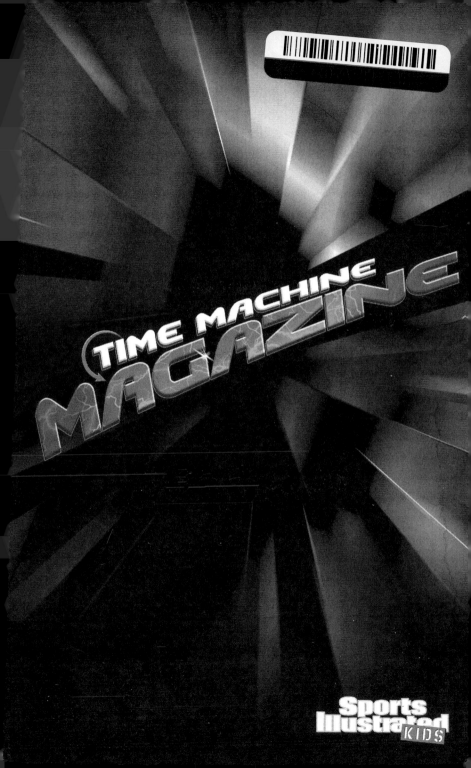

Time Machine Magazine books are published by Stone Arch Books
A Capstone Imprint
1710 Roe Crest Drive
North Mankato, Minnesota 56003
www.mycapstone.com

Library of Congress Cataloging-in-Publication Data is available on the Library of
Congress website.

ISBN 978-1-4965-2597-0 (library binding)
ISBN 978-1-4965-2706-6 (paperback)
ISBN 978-1-4965-2710-3 (ebook pdf)

Editor: Nate LeBoutillier
Designer: Ted Williams
Illustrator: Eduardo Garcia

Photo Credits: Sports Illustrated: Manny Millan, 124
Design Elements: Shutterstock

Printed in the United States of America in
Eau Claire, Wisconsin.
042016   009722R

TIME MACHINE MAGAZINE

GRIT and GOLD

BY BRANDON TERRELL

STONE ARCH BOOKS
a capstone imprint

"Conventional is not for me. I like things that are uniquely Flo. I like being different."

— Florence Griffith Joyner

CHAPTER 1

Rachel Young had always loved to run. Her dad used to joke that she'd gone straight from crawling to running, with no walking in between. "She has places to go," he'd say. "And she wants to get there fast."

But that was a long time ago. Before her parents separated. Before she and her mom moved back to Wells to live with her Grandpa Sam at the cabin on Clear Lake.

"Top three sprinters, hundred meters! Take your mark!" Coach Hartford's sharp voice carried across the track infield, followed by three quick chirps from her whistle. That was thirteen-year-old Rachel's cue. She was one of the fastest sprinters on the Wells Middle School track team. With the final conference meet of the track season fast approaching, it was her last time to show just how fast she could run.

Wells and the surrounding area were smack dab in the center of a stretch of hot days. The temperature outside was very close to cracking triple digits. The heat brought an extra layer of difficulty during practice.

Rachel took a few deep breaths and shook her legs out one at a time to loosen them before lining up alongside the other two sprinters who raced the 100 meters. To her left was Shelby Koua, a compact, no-nonsense runner. And to her right was Alyson Wainwright.

Alyson Wainwright made running look easy. She was so good at it, so good at *everything*, really, that she didn't even look like she was trying. Aly was tall—even taller than Rachel, and that was saying something. A burst of short red hair fell in curls around her face.

As the trio of racers silently prepared to enter the blocks, not even acknowledging each other, Rachel's mind drifted back to earlier that morning, to the cabin on Clear Lake.

Rachel had been speaking to her mom. The two stood in Rachel's makeshift bedroom, which was actually her grandpa's office. Her suitcase sat on the pullout futon bed, surrounded by a mountain of clothes. The rest of the room was not much cleaner. In fact, it looked like a tornado had struck it.

Rachel's mom had told her that she and Grandpa Sam were leaving on a road trip to Boston, where Rachel's dad still lived in a triple-decker apartment building in the Mission Hill neighborhood. It had

been a while since Rachel had been to the old, gray-brick building. While they were gone, Rachel would be staying in town with her cousin, Nate Winstead, and his parents.

Rachel dropped one last shirt into the suitcase and zipped it up. "Dad misses me, doesn't he?" she asked.

"Of course he does." Her mom ran a hand through Rachel's dark brown hair and smoothed it out. "And you'll visit him. Soon. But I have to sign some paperwork to finalize . . . you know."

The divorce, Rachel thought. *She just doesn't want to come right out and say it.*

"Grandpa Sam and I will be getting the rest of our things and bringing them back with us," her mom continued. "You won't even know we're gone."

Rachel doubted that.

"Come on," her mom said. "Aunt Holly and Uncle Peter are expecting us soon, so you and Nate can walk to school together."

Rachel lugged her suitcase off the bed, and she and her mom exited the minefield of a bedroom.

As they passed the stairs to the basement, Rachel paused ever so slightly. Before he retired, Grandpa Sam spent his entire career as a sports journalist. He'd interviewed famous athletes and traveled the world, bringing home a large collection of memorabilia that he now kept in the cabin's basement.

One important part of his collection was a file cabinet filled with old *Sports Illustrated* magazines.

They weren't ordinary magazines, though. Every so often, in a way that neither Rachel nor Nate had been able to understand, one of the magazines would glow blue and pulse with life. By reading an article out loud, the two teens had the power to travel in time to anywhere and any *when*.

With Grandpa Sam and her mom gone, the cabin and its magical contents would be locked away.

Grandpa Sam waited outside. The barrel-chested man leaned against the side of his four-door sedan. An empty trailer was hitched on to the back.

"Allow me," he said, his gruff voice boisterous and upbeat, as if he was trying to counter with joy how depressing the situation actually was. He took Rachel's suitcase from her and placed it into the trunk.

Rachel climbed into the back seat. As they backed out of the driveway, she cast the empty cabin one last, long look . . . .

"*On your mark!*"

Coach Hartford's order cut through the fog of memory. Rachel shook her head. She fitted her left foot into the block and placed her steepled fingers on the hot track. They stung, but she did not waver. The blazing sun beat down on the back of her neck.

"*Set!*"

The runners stilled and raised their haunches into the air.

Tweep!

Coach Hartford's whistle cut through the air.

Rachel shot out of the blocks, bursting forward as the breath hissed from her lungs. She pumped her arms and legs. The wind slipped across her face as she ran. Shelby dropped away, falling a few steps behind. But Aly surged ahead of Rachel, always ahead and never looking back. They hit the finish line and slowed to a jog. Rachel stopped and wiped her sweaty forehead with the bottom of her equally sweaty tank top.

"Great job, Aly!" Coach Hartford shouted, clapping loudly from her spot at the starting line. "The other sprinters won't know what hit 'em! Koua and Young, great effort, but I know you've got more in the tank!"

Rachel gave Coach Hartford a thumbs-up to let her know she'd been heard.

While another set of sprinters lined up to run, Rachel walked over to a nearby bench. A stack of towels sat next to a large orange cooler full of water. Rachel snatched a towel.

Shelby, Aly, and several other sprinters crowded together near the metal bleachers. Despite being teammates, Rachel was not great friends with any of the other girls. She kept her distance from them while staying close enough to hear their conversation.

"For real," Aly was saying. She had the rapt attention of the rest of the girls. "We're spending a whole week in Rome, then going up to Tuscany for another week. It's going to be the best family vacay ever."

"That sounds amazing," Shelby said, stone-faced.

"My parents just told me about it last night. Crazy cool, right?"

Rachel wiped her face again. "Yeah," she muttered under her breath. "Crazy."

As Rachel lined up for another practice sprint down the track, once again with lucky Aly and her perfect family life in the lane beside her, she thought about her own parents. About the last days in Boston when her dad was working late. About the times he finally would come home only to jump into an argument with her mom. About the moments Rachel could hear them yelling at each other through her bedroom walls. About the nights, when they thought she was fast asleep, that she'd bury her head under a pillow and cry.

Tweep!

The whistle caught Rachel off-guard. She leapt from the blocks, two steps behind Aly and the others. Hot tears began to sting the corners of her eyes and blur her vision. She fought them back, striding forward, putting her anger into her legs. She couldn't do it, though. She would never catch Aly Wainwright.

She lost ground and reached the finish line dead last. Unlike Aly and Shelby, though, Rachel didn't stop running. She passed them by and continued around the turn and onto the back of the track. It felt good to run. It felt *necessary*, just her and the track beneath her feet.

It felt like she could run forever.

She came to a stop on the far side of the track, away from the rest of the team. Rachel could feel their eyes on her, but she didn't care. She bent over and placed her hands on her knees.

Coach Hartford's voice drifted across the field. "Everything all right, Young?" she asked.

Rachel paused, then nodded. "Just fine, Coach!" she shouted back.

She hoped she sounded convincing enough.

Rachel caught up with Nate after practice. He and the rest of the boys' track team had spent their practice in the weight room, out of the sweltering heat.

"Hey, roomie!" he said. "How was practice? Anybody melt out there?"

"Shut it, you jerk," she said with a smile and a playful shove.

Nate's parents were parked and waiting for the two teens as they exited the school. When

Nate's dad saw them, he stepped out and walked around to greet them.

"Shall we?" Uncle Peter opened the back door of the car for them like he was a limo driver accommodating a wealthy client.

"It's Taco Night," Aunt Holly said from the passenger seat, her voice chipper and upbeat.

As they climbed into the backseat of the car, Nate leaned over to Rachel and whispered, "Sorry about them."

"It's cool," Rachel said. "I like tacos." A part of Rachel wanted to roll her eyes at the epic cheesiness of her aunt and uncle. But an even bigger part of her welcomed it, because it had been a long time since her *own* family felt whole, since she'd felt normal.

CHAPTER 2

Rachel stared at the contraption like it was something made by aliens and beamed down to Planet Earth. It annoyed her. It confused her. And even though she could run the 100-meter in under fifteen seconds, or perform a cast handstand on the uneven bars, or even *travel back in time*, she couldn't figure out how to work the evil thing in front of her.

"Are you just gonna have a staring contest with that sewing machine, Rach?" Nate chuckled from the desk next to her as he slid a piece of fabric under the needle of his own sewing machine and stepped on the pedal. He ran the fabric through with a whir.

The two teens were sitting in their second period family and consumer science class. Rachel was still tired from her first night of "sleep" at the Winstead house. The guest bedroom in the basement was nice and comfortable. It was the unfamiliar sounds—the creaking floors, the air conditioner rattling, cars driving past her window late at night—that kept Rachel awake. She hated that she didn't have her own bedroom anymore. Makeshift offices and guest bedrooms weren't enough. She needed a room of her own.

She needed a home.

Rows of long tables filled the FCS room. In front of each student was a sewing machine. Some kids looked as baffled as Rachel, while others were hunched over their machines, hard at work. Mrs. Laurence, the teacher, walked along inspecting each student's work. She had her hands behind her back and her black hair pulled into a ponytail.

Rachel grumbled under her breath. "Can't be *that* hard," she muttered. "Not if Nate can do it."

"I heard that," Nate said as he ran his fabric through on another pass.

So annoying, Rachel thought.

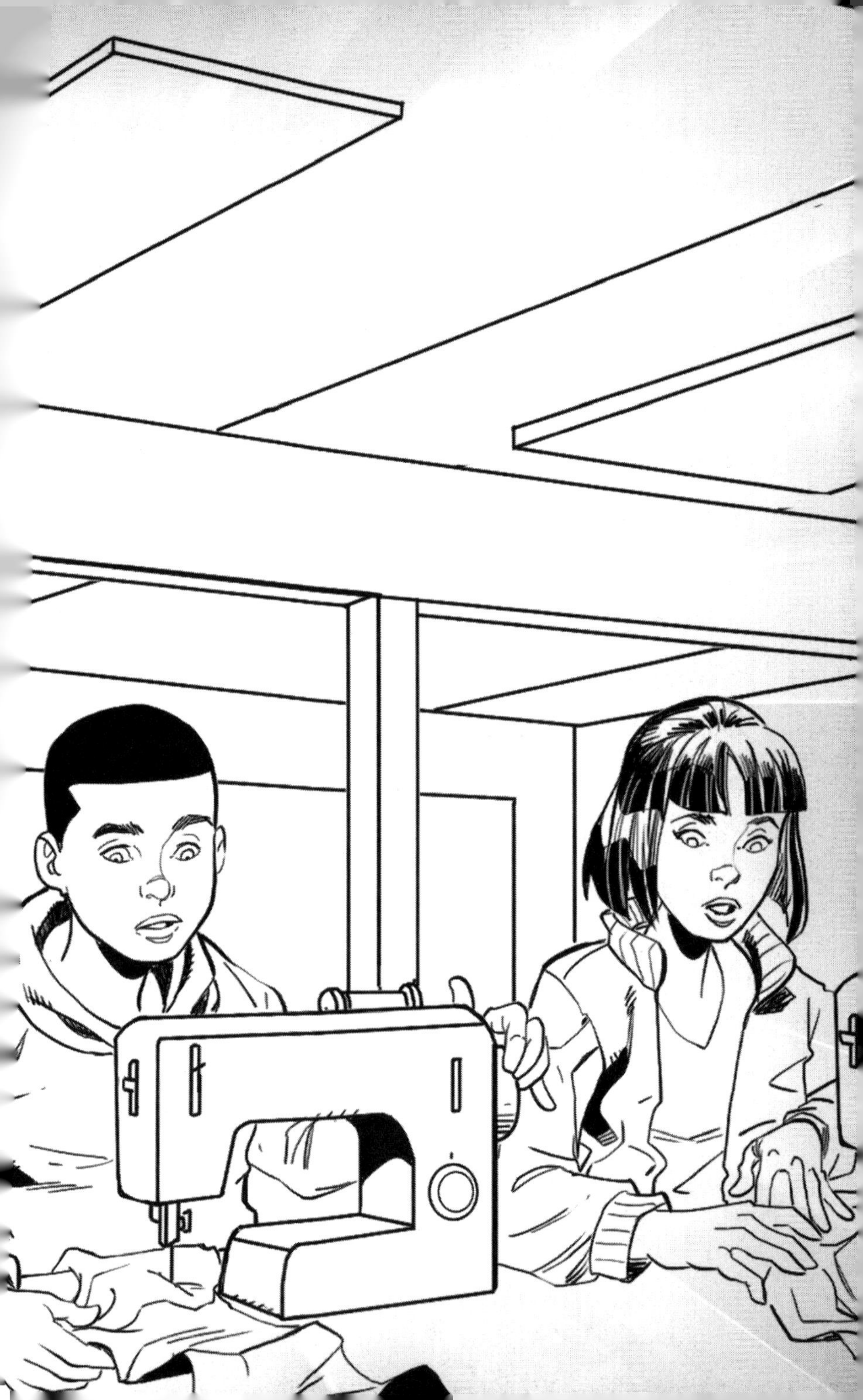

She picked up two scraps of blue fabric from beside her. Somehow she was supposed to sew the two pieces into one and create a pair of shorts. She lined the edge of the fabric scraps up with the needle and pressed her foot lightly down on the pedal.

It slowly began to move up and down.

See? Easy as a back handspring.

She moved the fabric toward the needle and thread with confidence. Rachel pressed down on the pedal, and the needle moved faster.

"You got this," she whispered to herself. "This is nothing."Rachel shifted in her seat, and her foot accidentally stomped the pedal. The sewing machine screamed like an accelerating jet engine, and the needle moved at ninja-level speed. Rachel threw her hands back as the fabric was whisked through and chewed up.

"Dang it!"

Rachel peeled her ruined project from the sewing machine. Her stitch looked like it belonged on Frankenstein's monster, not on a pair of shorts.

"Check these puppies out." Nate held his perfectly-stitched pair of shorts in front of him.

"Wonderful work, Nate," Mrs. Laurence cooed from one row over.

Nate beamed.

"Wonderful work, suck-up," a mocking voice chimed in from behind Rachel. Rachel turned in her chair to see Aly Wainwright doing her best impression of Mrs. Laurence.

Embarrassed, Nate went back to work on his project.

Aly locked eyes with Rachel and gave her a look that said, *What a dork*.

Rachel smiled.

By the end of class, Rachel's attempt at making a wearable pair of shorts had failed. Unless the person wearing them had an extra pair of legs. Or maybe two tails. She shoved the project into her cubby and fled the classroom.

The heat hit Rachel right in the face as she walked out of the girls' locker room, into the bright sun, and toward the middle school's track. She was dressed in a pair of shorts and the same blue and yellow Wells track team T-shirt as the rest of the girls.

"Rachel!" a voice called from behind her. "Wait up!"

Nate jogged up beside her, ready for practice. It looked like the boys would be outside braving the heat, then.

"No air-conditioned weight room today, huh?" Rachel said.

"Guess not," Nate said.

"Whatever are you going to do?" Rachel said sarcastically.

Nate shrugged. "Sweat. A lot."

"What a bummer!" Aly Wainwright's voice startled Rachel. She hadn't heard the track star approach. She turned to see Aly and Shelby behind them.

"I was hoping you'd wear those killer shorts you made in Mrs. Laurence's class today," Aly said to Nate with a giggle. "They were so stylish." She reached out and playfully nudged Nate in the shoulder.

"Well, uh . . . thanks . . . " he stammered. Like most boys, Nate's brain completely shut down when a pretty girl talked to him. Even if she was making fun of him without him realizing it.

Rachel realized it, though.

"I bet they'd look great on those scrawny turkey legs of yours," Aly added, twisting the knife. Her giggle turned into a full-on laugh. Even Shelby cracked a smile as Aly tucked her hands into her armpits like they were wings and pretended to be a turkey.

Nate's confused smile faded.

Aly looked over to Rachel to see what she thought of the joke. Rachel, who was short on friends and knew an invitation when she saw it, added, "Gobble, gobble."

Nate remained speechless.

Aly threw her head back and laughed. "Come on, Young," she said, draping an arm around Rachel's shoulder. The trio of girls walked in stride together toward the track, leaving Nate in their wake.

As they reached the infield, Rachel hazarded a glance over her shoulder. In the distance, she saw Nate walking alone toward the rest of the boys' track team. He looked like a lost puppy.

"So," Aly said, redirecting Rachel's attention back to her, "what are you doing after practice? Because we should totally hang out."

Even though she'd just turned her back on her cousin, Rachel felt something inside her leap. She was excited to have new friends.

To fit in at last.

CHAPTER 3

Rachel, Aly, and a few other girls went to Aly's favorite restaurant to eat. A Taste of Rome was a small Italian place "with the best spaghetti you've ever eaten," according to Aly. Rachel thought it was all right, but nothing compared to Mama Carla's, the hole-in-the-wall Italian place her family used to frequent in Boston.

"The meatballs!" her dad would shout at the top of his lungs every time they left, a family tradition, shaking his fists toward the sky. "*The meatballs!*"

But A Taste of Rome was good enough. Besides, Rachel didn't really care about the food. She was more excited to hang out with Aly and her friends.

From the restaurant, they walked to the neighboring mall. They meandered around, marveling at the sharply-dressed mannequins in the store windows and poking fun at the other patrons as they shopped. Aly told most of the jokes. Some were funny, others kind of mean. The rest of the girls just laughed and played along.

By the time Aly's mom dropped Rachel off at Uncle Peter and Aunt Holly's house, it was after nine o'clock.

Aly gave her a quick hug. "I'm so glad you came to hang out with us," she said, a heartfelt, genuine compliment.

"Yeah," Rachel said. "Me, too."

She passed the Winsteads in the living room, where the three were watching a cooking competition show. Nate sat on the floor, surrounded by books and writing in a notebook. He didn't look up. On the television screen, an angry chef was yelling at the rest of the staff.

"Welcome home," Aunt Holly said with a smile.

Uncle Peter patted the empty spot on the couch beside him. "Pull up a cushion," he said with his usual level of pep.

Rachel shook her head. "No thanks," she said. "I'm gonna call it a night."

She breezed through the living room. Nate finally glanced up but said nothing. He still looked super upset.

Rachel hurried down the steps to her basement room, hoping he didn't follow her to question her about how she'd thrown him under the bus earlier.

Thankfully, he didn't.

Nate's silent treatment extended to the following morning's car ride to school. The two teens sat together in the backseat while, up front, Uncle Peter quietly listened to sports talk radio.

Neither spoke until they walked into the cafeteria of Wells Middle School and Nate sarcastically said, "There's Aly and her flock of sheep!" He pointed to a table, where Aly, Shelby, and a few others sat together.

"Knock it off, Nate," Rachel said.

Aly looked up, saw Rachel, and waved her over.

Rachel hurried along. Behind her, Nate called out, "Bye! Enjoy making fun of people! *Baa, baa!*"

She tried to ignore him.

When Rachel reached the table of girls, Shelby slid over to make room for her. She plunked down her backpack and sat.

"Aly really thinks that we should have a team get-together," Shelby said, trying to get Rachel up to speed on the conversation.

Aly slammed both hands down on the table in excitement. "We don't have school Friday," she said. "And it's the day before the last meet of the season. So we should celebrate by totally having a team party."

Before Rachel could stop herself, she blurted out, "My grandpa is out of town. We can have it at his cabin." She didn't know exactly why she said it. Probably because she really wanted the girls—most importantly, Aly—to like her.

It was like she'd just offered them a million dollars. The girls around the table perked up and began to whisper to one another.

"Really?" Aly leaned forward.

"That would be amazing," said one of the girls, a blonde named Jerrika Holmes.

"Yes!" Aly shouted. "The whole girls' team. Maybe a few others."

"Great idea, Aly," Jerrika said.

"I know," Aly said. "It's perfect. Right, Rachel?"

Rachel opened her mouth, but didn't know what to say. Her tumbling snowball had just rolled into an avalanche. Finally, she said, "Yeah. It'll be perfect."

It took until the end of the school day for Nate to catch wind of Rachel's plan. She was at her locker, cramming books into her backpack before heading to track practice, when he strode up next to her.

"A party?" It was a question that wasn't really a question. "You're having a party? At Grandpa Sam's? What are you thinking?"

Rachel shrugged. "Be cool. It's just gonna be the track team hanging out."

Nate laughed. "Ha! Yeah, right."

"How did you find out anyway?"

"History class. Jerrika spent half of Mr. Colby's lecture sending texts about it."

Hearing this made Rachel's stomach flip over. "Well, I'll keep it under control."

"Rachel, it's bad enough that Grandpa Sam and your mom aren't there, but what if someone goes into the basement? What if they find Grandpa's *Sports Illustrated* collection?"

"Nate," Rachel said. "Calm down. That's not gonna happen. I won't let anyone go near those magazines."

"You better not."

Slinging her backpack onto her shoulder, Rachel said, "Just don't tell your parents I'm going out to the cabin Thursday night, okay?"

Nate didn't answer.

"*Okay?*" Rachel repeated.

He still said nothing, just nodded quickly.

Rachel walked off down the hall, heading for track practice without waiting for Nate to catch up.

CHAPTER 4

In the nights that followed, Rachel spent her time in the Winstead's basement, doing homework or watching television on her phone. When Uncle Peter asked if anything was wrong, she pulled the whole "I just miss my mom" card out of her back pocket. Worked every time.

Of course, she *did* miss her mom. She spoke to her once on the phone, on Wednesday night. She and Grandpa Sam had been gone for three days.

"See you Friday after practice, love," her mom said. She sounded tired. "Be good."

"You know me," Rachel answered, thinking of Aly and the party.

She spent her after-school hours on the track, preparing for the meet. When she raced alone, her mind was clear and her times were right on target. But not when Aly, who would also be racing in the

100-meter at the meet, ran side-by-side with her. The natural athlete was intimidating, and her presence alone threw Rachel off. She didn't have the grit and tenacity to keep pace with Aly. She couldn't race her best, and she knew it.

Unfortunately, Coach Hartford knew it, too.

"Try it again, Young!" she yelled, blowing her whistle and making Rachel come back to the starting line. "You're picking up your head, and it's affecting your speed!"

Rachel tried, but she couldn't focus on the track, or on the finish line. She was thinking too much.

At the end of practice on Thursday, Coach Hartford approached her. She sat beside Rachel on the metal bleachers. "It's not easy being the new kid," she said. "I get it. I've been there myself. I was an Army brat. My family moved to a new town almost every year. New school, new kids. It was tough."

"Yeah," was all Rachel could say.

"Whatever's happening off the track, leave it there. If you want to win, you need to stay focused and confident. I have faith in you."

That makes one of us, Rachel thought.

Clear Lake was two miles outside of Wells. Rachel biked there after practice, duffel bag slung over her handlebars. Her legs burned from a tiring week on the track, and it was still hot and cloudless, the wind feeling more like hot breath than a refreshing breeze. The trek to Grandpa Sam's cabin was anything but comfortable.

The cabin was draped in shadows from the thicket of trees surrounding it. The place looked peaceful, but also slightly eerie. She'd never been there alone before.

"Relax," she told herself. "It's still the same old cabin."

Grandpa Sam kept an extra key under a potted plant on the porch.

"Hello?" she called out as she entered, as if expecting someone to answer.

In the kitchen, she rummaged through the pantry and cabinets in search of snacks. She was pretty sure her friends were planning on bringing their own stuff, but she didn't want to seem like an unwelcoming host.

All she could find, though, was a bag of half-eaten pretzels, some spreadable cheese and crackers, and six cans of root beer.

It'll have to do, she thought as she placed them all on the kitchen island.

The doorbell rang at seven-thirty as the sun began to set across the lake. Rachel swung the door open to find Aly, Shelby, and Jerrika standing there.

Aly spread her arms wide. "This place is *killer*," she said, bustling past Rachel and taking in the whole cabin. "I love it. So rustic and cool. I'm crazy jealous."

Shelby lugged two plastic bags in her hands. They were filled with snack food—rice cakes and veggie chips. She dropped them off on the kitchen island, right next to Rachel's paltry supply of snacks.

Soon after, two other track teammates showed up, followed by another girl Rachel didn't really know. She wasn't on the team but seemed to know Jerrika pretty well.

They ate and talked in the kitchen. Rachel had to admit that the gathering of track teammates was more low-key than she'd imagined.

And then the doorbell rang.

"The boys are here!" Aly squealed, racing to the door and flinging it open.

"Boys?" Rachel didn't remember inviting boys.

Suddenly, the cabin was flooded with people as several boys from Wells Middle School showed up. She recognized a few from the track team—Kyle Laughlin, Joe Rathburn, Mike Deemer.

Jerrika found Grandpa Sam's record player in the living room and shouted, "Vintage vinyls!" She dug out a record, cranked up the volume, and old, scratchy rock and roll blasted through the speaker.

This is terrible! thought Rachel. She looked around like she was standing at a disaster site. What had started as a simple party had gotten out of control in a matter of minutes.

"How cool is this?" Aly asked her, shouting into Rachel's ear to be heard.

Rachel tried to keep her composure. "So cool."

"You rock, Young!"

A blood-curdling scream erupted from the living room. Rachel and the others in the kitchen bustled over to see what was the matter.

Jerrika stood pointing at the window. "There's somebody outside!" she shrieked, acting like she was in a horror movie.

A face peered in through the window. Rachel identified it right away.

Nate!

Bubbling with a combination of anger and embarrassment, Rachel stormed out of the door and stalked around the cabin until she reached the lakeside living room windows. "Nate?!" she bellowed.

Nate, still standing by the windows, threw his hands into the air.

"What are you doing out here?!" Rachel shouted.

"I was just checking—" Nate started, then stopped. "I thought this was a *little* get-together."

"Well . . . plans change."

"Wait until Grandpa Sam finds out."

"You wouldn't." Rachel, fists balled in anger, prepared to really yell at Nate. But instead, she stopped and looked toward the window. A trio of faces peered back at her through the glass.

"Come on," she said, grabbing Nate by the arm.

She led him inside the house, where the partygoers could see him. Kyle Laughlin laughed. "Hey," he said. "It's Nate Winstead, professional party pooper."

Rachel hauled Nate down the steps and into Grandpa Sam's dark basement. She didn't even bother to click on any light; the blue moonlight glowing through the windows was enough to see by.

"Do you know how embarrassing this is?" Rachel hissed.

"I don't care," Nate said.

"I do! Because I'm finally fitting in, finally making friends at this stupid school."

"And I wasn't your friend?"

"No. You're my cousin, Nate!"

The silence that followed hung heavy and thick in the air. Suddenly a flicker of blue light danced at the corner of Rachel's eye. It was quick, but it made her heart flutter.

"Did you see that?" Nate asked.

"No," she lied.

A second, longer burst of blue light rippled through the dark basement.

"Yes!" Nate pumped a fist. "It's the file cabinet, Rachel. One of Grandpa Sam's old *Sports Illustrated* magazines."

As much as Rachel loved traveling in time, this was quite possibly the worst moment for it to happen. She begrudgingly followed Nate across the basement to the old wooden file cabinet. He seemed to have forgotten their argument.

A small key was stuck in the top drawer. Nate twisted it and pulled the drawer out. Strands of bright blue energy shot out from the cabinet like they'd been trapped inside and were finally free.

"Where is it?" Nate whispered as he rifled through the magazines, searching for the source of the energy.

Rachel looked at the stairs. She hoped no one was spying on them. The bass and rhythm of the music from the record player made the ceiling above her rattle.

"Here!" Nate plucked a magazine from the cabinet, and the blue energy snaked around his fingers, up his wrist and forearm.

"Nate, we can't time-travel right now," Rachel said. "Not with everyone upstairs."

"Remember," Nate said, "When we get back, no time at all will have passed. It'll be like we never left."

He was right, but still, she hated to risk it. "Can we wait until after the party?"

As if to answer her, the sparks spitting off the magazine leaped over to her, like they were drawing her in.

Rachel's curiosity got the best of her. In the blue glow, she tried hard to see what was on the cover of the *Sports Illustrated* in Nate's hands.

Two African-American women in red-and-white leotards smiled back at her. Numerous medals hung around their necks. In the right corner was

the five-ring symbol of the Olympic Games. At
the top of the magazine was a title in bold letters.
"*America's Golden Girls*," Nate read aloud from the
magazine's cover.

Rachel stepped closer. Now she was interested.
"Florence Joyner and Jackie Joyner-Kersee?"

"Looks like we're about to see ourselves some
more track and field," Nate said. "Let's hope it's
not as . . . *dangerous* as 1936 Berlin."

Rachel thought back to their first experience
time-traveling, not that long ago. They'd jumped
back to Nazi Germany to watch Jesse Owens
compete in the Summer Games. A Nazi guard had
nearly trapped them in 1936.

Nate opened the magazine. As he was about
to read, a strand of blue energy spun around the
magazine and flipped it closed.

"Whoa!" said Nate. "That's never happened!"

"This isn't a good idea, Nate," Rachel said.

From the top of the steps, Aly yelled, "Hey,
Rachel! Everything cool?!"

"Yeah!" Rachel yelled back. "Up in a minute!"

Someone laughed, and a girl's voice said, "Once she's done dealing with her weird creeper cousin."

A round of laughter followed.

Rachel wasn't sure if Nate heard. He was watching the blue energy stretch like gum from the *Sports Illustrated* in his hands back toward the file cabinet. "It's almost like the magazine is attached to something," he said. "Here."

Nate thrust the *SI* into Rachel's hands. Goosebumps blossomed like a wave down her arms and up her spine as she watched Nate follow the blue energy back toward the cabinet.

"It *is* attached to another magazine," he said, like he was Sherlock Holmes solving a particularly difficult mystery. He reached into the file cabinet and withdrew a second *Sports Illustrated*. As he did, the energy snaked around it. The two magazines were tied together.

"*U.S. Olympic Trials*," Nate read. "*Fastest Woman in the World*."

The second *SI* also featured Florence Joyner on the cover. This time, she was mid-stride, wearing a blue singlet that continued down one leg. Both arms were raised to the sky. Her index fingers—with their bright red nail polish—pointed upward.

"The Olympic Trials," Rachel said. "That's when she broke the 100-meter dash record."

"Smashed it," Nate said, pointing to the *SI* cover. "At least, that's how they put it."

He spread open the magazine, searching out the article. As he did, Rachel stopped him. "Wait," she said. "Nate, this is stupid. We can't go." She pointed up at the ceiling.

The bass-thumping music continued.

"It'll be fine," Nate argued. Before she could stop him, he began to read from the article. "*Get up and go*," he read. "*Florence Griffith Joyner's dramatic garb made her a colorful blur as she smashed the world record in the 100 at the Olympic trials.*" The blue energy intensified and wrapped around them.

Rachel looked around the basement. Suddenly
the world shifted and spun. It became hazy and
out of focus, like they were standing in the eye
of a storm. Three brilliant flashes of light erupted

from the magazine, and blue tendrils of energy snaked around them.

And then, in an instant, everything went black.

CHAPTER 5

The party was gone.

The music was gone.

The dark basement was gone.

It was bright and hot, and Rachel felt like she was going to pass out.

This wasn't the first time she and Nate had time-traveled, but every time they did, the extreme change in location caught her off-guard. This time was no different. The thick, humid air that swirled and blew around her was heavy and hard to breathe.

Rachel doubled over and coughed. She still clutched the *Sports Illustrated* with Florence Joyner and Jackie Joyner-Kersee on the cover. She could sense Nate beside her and imagined he was going through the same motion sickness.

"Wow," Nate said, followed by a cough of his own. "Looking sharp, cuz."

Rachel's jeans and purple shirt had been replaced by a neon pink leotard that sparkled in the sunlight. Baby blue tights covered her legs, and her hair was pulled back by a shiny headband.

"Oh, no!" she exclaimed in horror. "What am I wearing?"

Nate, who had on a simple tie-dye T-shirt and a pair of baggy shorts, shrugged his shoulders. "Looks like a track outfit," he said.

Apparently, Nate's love of history and adventure had trumped his anger over the party. But even though they'd traveled miles and *years* from the party at Grandpa Sam's cabin, Rachel was still annoyed with her cousin. "Where are we?" she grumbled.

They were outside, hidden under the shade of a tall tree on the side of a road. A car zipped past, an old station wagon with its windows down, blasting music. Behind her, she could hear the low rumble of a crowd.

An amplified voice on a sound system echoed through the air, and Rachel turned toward the noise. Across the street and past a fence was a large stadium. Several sets of floodlights stretched into the blue sky around it. The rows of bleachers were packed.

"Wait," Rachel said. "I think we're at the 1988 Olympic trials."

"The ones on the cover of the *SI*," Nate said, holding up the magazine featuring Joyner crossing the finish line. "So what exactly are the trials?"

"The best athletes in the country have to qualify for the Olympic team," Rachel explained. She checked for traffic and crossed the street. Nate followed. She stood at the fence, peering in. "I think this is where Florence Joyner broke the world record."

"Smashed," Nate corrected her, pointing at the magazine's headline.

"Come on," he said as he began to walk the length of the fence. "We have to get inside to watch."

Rachel followed, annoyed and wishing she could hide her outfit. They made their way around the perimeter of the stadium. Loud swells of cheers filled the air. Nate flipped through one of the *Sports Illustrated* magazines. "What do you know about Florence Joyner?" he asked.

"She's the most decorated female sprinter in U.S. Olympic history," Rachel answered. "She still holds the Olympic records in both the women's 100- and 200-meter dashes. She was also known for her fancy fingernails and the wild outfits she used to wear."

"Like that one?" Nate nodded at the leotard Rachel wore.

She squirmed uncomfortably. "Yeah, I guess."

Nate snatched the *Sports Illustrated* out of Rachel's hand. He fumbled with holding two magazines. "How many medals did she win?" he asked.

"In 1988?" Rachel shrugged. "I dunno. Three, I think?"

He pointed at the cover of Rachel's magazine, the one featuring the two dynamic sprinters. "Three golds and a silver," he said.

They'd reached the entrance of the stadium. A crowd of people milled about. Rachel actually didn't feel too out of place anymore with her crazy leotard. She noticed that most people in 1988 wore outfits as wild as hers. Acid-washed denim shorts. Baggy shirts in bright colors. Oversize hats or hair that poofed out and was stuck in place with a full can of hairspray. A man walked past wearing a red shirt that read *Don't Worry, Be Happy*.

Rachel shook her head in amazement.

"Wow!" a voice said from behind them. "That outfit is totally radical."

Spinning on a heel, Rachel discovered a teenage girl standing behind them. She was older than she and Nate by a year or two. The girl was tall and pretty, with mocha skin and thick, curly black hair. She wore an outrageous

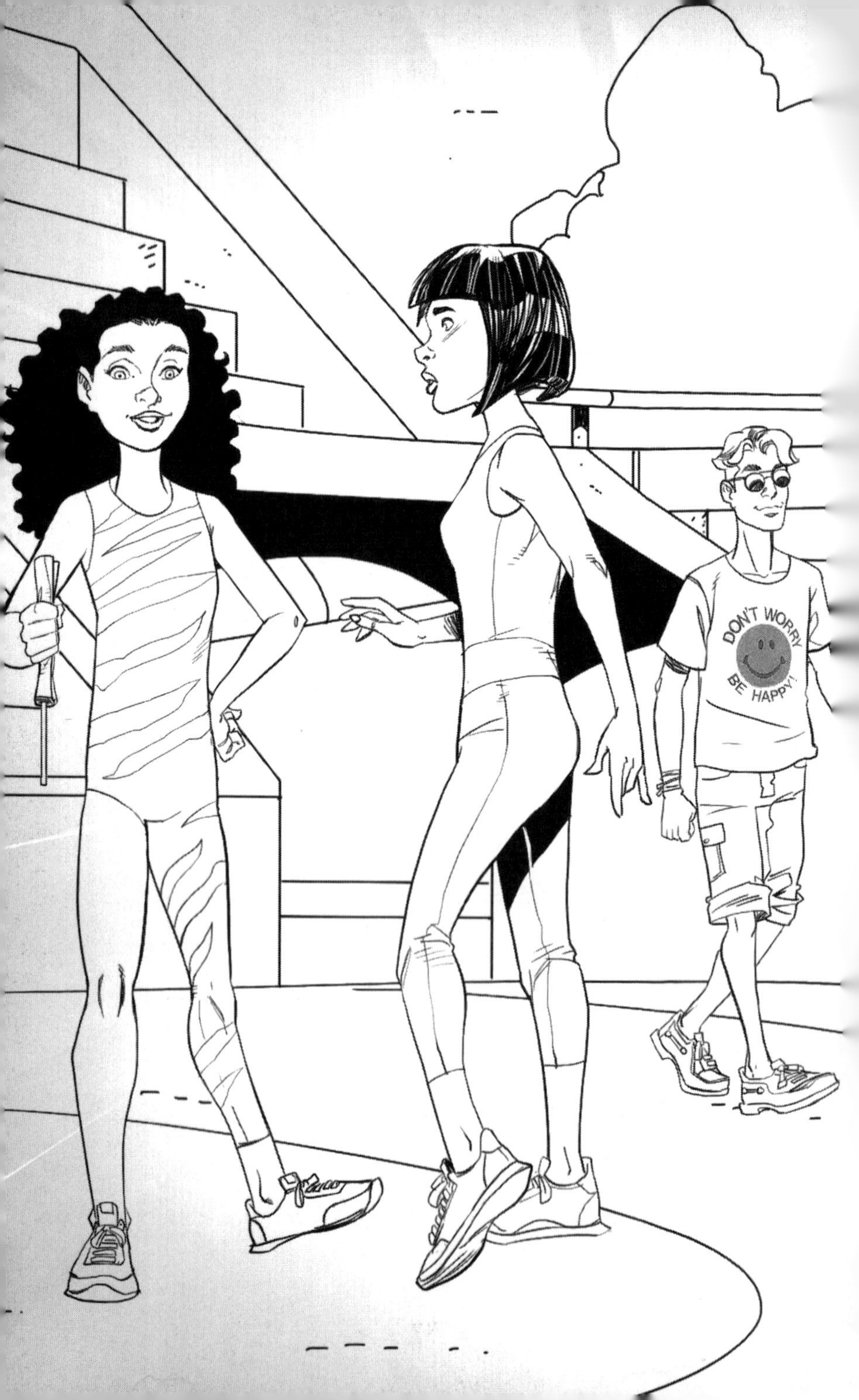
DON'T WORRY
BE HAPPY!

leotard of her own: It was red and yellow striped. The leotard covered one leg, leaving the other exposed. She held a large, rolled-up sign in one hand.

"Uh, thanks," Rachel said. "You, too."

The girl gave her a wide smile. "Thanks. Name's Maya. Maya Gordon."

"I'm Rachel."

Nate opened his mouth, but no words came out. He was staring at Maya like a puppy dog.

Rachel elbowed him. "This is Nate, my drooling cousin."

Maya laughed.

Rachel nodded to the sign in Maya's hands. "What's that?" she asked.

Maya unrolled the large, heavy-duty paper and held it with both hands. The sign was written in big bubble letters. It read: *FLO JO IS #1!!!*

"What's a Flo Jo?" Nate asked.

"Not what," Maya said. "*Who.* Florence Joyner, dweeb. Flo. Jo. She's, like, an icon. It's so gnarly to run into another Florence Joyner fan who dressed up. Did you see what she was wearing here yesterday? It was so tubular."

Gnarly? Tubular? Rachel felt like she needed a guidebook of 1980s slang to understand what Maya was saying.

Nate looked confused. "Why do people care what she wears?"

Maya tucked her sign back under one arm, grabbed Nate with the other, and led him through the crowd without saying a word. Rachel followed close behind. They reached a waist-high barrier that looked out at the sea of athletes just as a voice over the sound system said, "Women's 100-meter final. Racers to their mark."

Maya pointed out at the athletes as they shed their shirts and warm-up outfits. "Can you tell which one is Flo Jo?" she asked. "It should be easy."

Nate still looked confused. It was kind of his default expression, though. "The . . . one in blue?" he finally said.

"Right," the girl said. "The one that stands out. The one that's *unique*." Rachel had to admit, Maya had a point. Flo Jo was wearing the same outfit from the second *Sports Illustrated* Nate had pulled from the cabinet in Grandpa Sam's basement.

As they watched, the racers in each lane were announced. When they announced the woman in lane five, a tall sprinter named Evelyn Ashford, Maya said, "Ashford is Flo Jo's biggest threat. The top three racers will go on to compete in Seoul, so Flo Jo's got this in the bag."

Florence Joyner was announced in lane six. She stood with her hands on her hips, staring down at the finish line.

"Quiet for the start, please," said the announcer. A wave of silence washed over the stadium as the runners took their place in the starting blocks.

Rachel leaned closer, like the Olympic all-star's appeal was magnetic.

Bang!

The starter pistol echoed through the stadium. The racers darted out of the blocks as the crowd noise rose again. "Come on, Flo Jo!" Maya shouted from beside Rachel. She held up her sign, waving it back and forth.

Joyner surged ahead of the pack, moving with grace and agility. Beside her, Evelyn Ashford kept stride.

Maya was right; Joyner was the woman to beat. Halfway down the track, she broke loose of her competition, and she crossed the finish line with one arm raised high in victory.

"Whoa!" Maya pointed to the racers' unofficial time on a towering black scoreboard. Beside Joyner's name was a time of 10.61 seconds. "She broke the world record! The previous record was, like, 10.8. Radical!"

On the track, Joyner collapsed to the ground in celebration. Evelyn Ashford, who'd taken second place, joined her. A woman named Jennifer Inniss was announced as the third place winner.

Rachel spied a man in a white polo shirt weaving through the crowd. Maya must have seen him, too. "There's Al Joyner," she said. "Flo Jo's husband and trainer!"

Al scooped Flo Jo off the track and into his arms.

Rachel looked over and saw Nate jump a bit, like he'd been stung by a bee or bitten by a bug. *Or zapped by electricity*. A small gasp escaped his lips, and he quickly hid the magazine behind his back.

"Is everything okay?" Maya asked. She hadn't noticed the flicker of blue light dancing behind Nate.

"Yeah," Rachel said. "We . . . uh, we have to go."

"But we just met," Maya said. "Bummer."

Rachel discovered she was a bit bummed out, too. She liked their new friend.

"Are you sure?" Maya was doing everything she could to get them to stay.

"We're sure." Nate's voice quivered as another tendril of energy wrapped around his hand and arm.

Maya sighed. "Fine," she said. "Guess I'll see ya later."

I wish, Rachel thought.

She and Nate left the stadium while Florence Joyner was still basking in her 100-meter dash victory and raced out onto the street. When they found the tall trees from before, the blue energy from the *Sports Illustrated* in Nate's hand grew to encompass him.

"We're going back already?" Rachel asked. Their stay had been so quick. Not like the other times. The blue energy twined down Nate's arm, around him, until it swirled around Rachel, as well. A wave of strength and adrenaline hit her, and she could feel her pulse rate quicken, could practically feel her heart thudding in her chest.

Immediately, the world around them began to shift.

Like clockwork, three brilliant flashes of light erupted. In an instant, everything went black.

CHAPTER 6

This isn't Grandpa Sam's cabin. This place smells like . . . fish?

Rachel opened her eyes and tried to gather her surroundings. She was in a sea of people, all bustling around her, unconcerned with her confusion and fear. Nate was at her side, though. They were in some kind of outdoor fish market. Rows of vendors sold fresh fish and seafood. Tanks brimmed with eels and octopi and lobsters.

Rachel wrinkled her nose. *Ew*, she thought.

She sighed relief when she discovered she was no longer wearing the ridiculous leotard. It had been replaced by a red polo shirt and gray shorts. Nate wore something similar, only his shirt was bright blue. He had a bag slung over one shoulder, which he slid the two magazines into before zipping it shut.

The handwritten market signs featured beautiful, sweeping characters in a language Rachel could not read. She didn't have to read them to know where they were, though.

"We're in South Korea," she said.

Seoul, to be exact. And if history had a way of repeating itself, then any minute, she or Nate would see—

"Look!" Nate pointed to a row of posters glued to a wooden wall of the fish market. They featured a running man carrying a torch, along with the words *Seoul 1988*. Above the man, radiating brilliant lines like they were glowing with sunlight, were the five Olympic rings.

"We didn't go back to Grandpa Sam's cabin because of this," Nate said. He held up the second issue of *Sports Illustrated* he'd taken from the file cabinet, the one that featured Florence Joyner and Jackie Joyner-Kersee on the cover.

A man carrying a paper bag overflowing with crab legs bumped into Rachel. As he quietly apologized and continued on his way, Rachel said, "Let's get out of this crowd."

They wove through the mass of market-goers. Nate craned his neck. "Why did we jump *here*, of all places? Why not right by the Olympic stadium or something?"

As if in answer, a squeal of delight pierced the air. It was followed by a girl's voice saying, "Holy cow! Is it really you?"

Rachel's heart swelled. She turned. Sure enough, standing there among the crowd was Maya, a brightly-colored beacon in a sea of gray.

"Maya!" Rachel ran up to the girl. Her vibrant clothes made her hard to miss. She wore a sequined dress with a neon pink sweater over it and a pair of Converse sneakers.

"It *is* you!" Maya dropped the paper bag she was carrying and wrapped Rachel in a hug, like they were old friends instead of only having met once. "You guys just up and disappeared in Indianapolis. What happened?"

"It's . . . hard to explain," Rachel said. For Maya, it had been a couple of months since she'd seen Nate and Rachel. But to the two time-traveling teens, it had been just minutes.

"Are you here to watch the Olympics?" Maya asked as she picked up her bag of groceries. "Oh, who am I kidding? Of course you are."

The trio began to walk through the market. They made their way out onto the streets of Seoul. Around them, tall buildings stretched to the sky. It was mid-afternoon, and bright sunlight filtered through, casting harsh shadows across metal and glass.

"Daddy and I are staying right on the Han River, in the Grand Seoul Hotel," Maya said. "Where are you guys staying?"

Rachel looked at Nate. "We . . . uh, we haven't booked a room yet," she said.

Maya gasped. "You haven't?"

"Well, it's kind of just the two of us, and . . . ." Again, Rachel didn't know how to explain their situation.

"Never fear, Maya is here. You'll stay with Daddy and me. He's never around anyway. Too busy with work. So I fend for myself." She held up the paper bag. "Like buying my own dinner. I was sick of room service. Come on."

Maya led the way, crossing at the next intersection before turning right and heading straight. She reminded Rachel of Aly Wainwright, so fiercely confident. Rachel sped up until she was in stride with Maya. Nate lagged behind, alone.

They walked along the bank of the river, where Rachel could see long bridges spanning across to the far side. This section of the city had less skyscrapers, more thickets of trees.

"Is that the Olympic Stadium?" Nate asked.

Perched on the far side of the riverbank was an enormous arena with swooping architecture. The fluid metal structure looked like a wave in motion.

"Yep," Maya said, all nonchalant. "Jamsil Olympic Stadium."

"Duh," Rachel said, scoffing at Nate.

Nate either didn't hear or ignored her. "This is a great view," he said.

"Just wait," Maya said. "I'll get you a better view."

The Grand Seoul Hotel had a crimson awning and glass doors framed in shimmering gold. It was by far the ritziest hotel Rachel had ever seen. They walked through a set of revolving doors into a massive lobby with a crystal chandelier hanging from the ceiling.

"Whoa," Nate whispered.

Maya strode through the lobby like she owned the place. Rachel's mind was officially boggled. When they'd met the Flo Jo-crazy teen in Indianapolis, she'd had no idea Maya was so . . . well, so *rich*.

A special key was required to operate the elevator. Maya casually inserted one into the elevator and pressed the top button. "Penthouse, here we come," she said.

The elevator rose so fast and far that Rachel imagined it busting out of the top of the hotel. Finally, they slowed. The door *pinged* and slid open.

The penthouse was stunning. Rich, ornate furniture filled the space, as well as two enormous beds so big they could fit a family of slumbering giants. A smaller chandelier to match the one in the lobby hung above it. There was a dining area, a large television, a hot tub near the bathroom, and a wall of windows revealing the blue skies of South Korea.

"Wow." Rachel was dumbfounded. She'd never experienced luxury like this before.

"So this is how the other half lives," Nate whispered. He walked over to the windows and pressed his hands and forehead against the glass like he was a toddler. "Hey! Jamsil Stadium!"

"Told you I'd show you a better view," Maya said with a smirk.

"Nate," Rachel said. "Stop slobbering up the glass." She chuckled and looked at Maya. "I can't take him anywhere."

Nate wiped the window clean with his hand. "Sorry," he said.

They sat at the oversized table and ate. Maya had purchased more than enough for all of them, like she'd known they would be joining her for dinner. As they ate, the sun lowered in the sky, casting the Olympic stadium in fiery colors and shadows.

"I can't believe the Opening Ceremony is tomorrow," Maya said.

"We'll have great seats," Nate mumbled, his mouth filled with a seaweed and rice roll called a *gimbap*. He pointed a thumb over his shoulder at the window.

"Yeah," Maya said, a sly twinkle in her eye. "We will."

"Rise and shine!" Maya's voice sang out.

Rachel peeled her eyes open. It was the following morning. She'd fallen asleep in one of the mammoth beds the night before while they watched television. Nate was beside her, also crawling up from dreamland.

Maya was already dressed in another colorful, memorable outfit. This time it was a purple jumpsuit and a pair of green high tops. Her curly hair had been pulled into twin pom-poms on either side of her head. Something was dangling from her outstretched hand. Two items, hanging on cords.

"What are they?" Rachel croaked.

Maya tossed the items onto the bed. Rachel clawed at one of them. It was a lanyard with a laminated pass attached. The pass had the five Olympic rings on it, along with the words: *ALL ACCESS*.

Rachel was instantly awake. "No way," she said.

"Yep." Maya smiled. "Daddy pulled some strings and got me two extras. He's already awake and gone to a meeting or something."

Rachel had fallen asleep before Maya's father had gotten back to the hotel room.

Maya offered Rachel a red- and blue-striped dress to wear while Nate was forced to wear the same clothes he'd worn the day before.

She caught him sniffing his shirt to see how dirty it was.

"Nate," she said. "Don't be so gross."

The teens ordered room service for breakfast. It was nearly lunch, but that didn't stop Rachel from getting a pile of pancakes shaped like the Leaning Tower of Pisa.

Finally, the door to the hotel room opened, and a towering man in an expensive linen suit entered. His bald head gleamed, and a wide smile crossed his lips.

"Daddy!" Maya shouted.

"Hey, darling," he said. "Are these your new friends?"

Maya introduced her dad to Nate and Rachel. Rachel liked Mr. Gordon right away. He looked her in the eye when she spoke to him, like he was hanging on her every word.

"So," Mr. Gordon said, rubbing his hands together in anticipation. "Are you kids ready for the Opening Ceremony?"

"Yeah!" they all shouted in unison.

Mr. Gordon led the way across the packed streets of Seoul. People from around the globe had traveled to see the festivities. *Sure*, Rachel thought, *but none of them traveled from the future to watch*.

The passes around their necks allowed them to enter the stadium from a set of side doors. Men and women in expensive clothing walked alongside them. Mr. Gordon knew several of them, taking time to shake their hands.

"I can't believe you're wearing that," Rachel said to Nate, noticing that his outfit and shoulder bag were horribly out of place among the elite guests.

"Uh, what was I *supposed* to wear?" Nate asked, confused.

Rachel did not respond. She hurried along to sidle up next to Maya.

They sat near the center of the stadium. Traditional Korean drums thundered and echoed from the grassy infield. Their rhythmic sound filled the entire arena.

Rachel watched in awe as dancers and flag bearers carried colorful banners onto the infield. They twirled and rotated, creating a large 88 in honor of the year. They twisted and danced until they first spelled out the word *WELCOME* and then the Olympic rings with a flickering swoop of color above them.

The procession of athletes followed, and Rachel was finally able to see Florence Joyner for the first time.

The athlete wore a blue and white jumpsuit like the rest of the team, and she waved a small American flag back and forth.

When the teams had passed through the arena, the music and dancers began again.

"Look!" Nate pointed to the sky, where five parachutes had unfurled above the stadium. Blue. Yellow. Black. Green. Red. They glided down to the infield grass to the roar of the crowd.

The dancing continued for a long time until a flock of white doves were released into the sky. They swooped and dove and flew through the air. Two South Koreans—one a gold medalist in the 1936 Games, the other a famous athlete—each carried an Olympic torch through the stadium. They passed the torches on to a trio of young athletes, who were then raised into the air alongside a massive pedestal with a bowl at the top.

They touched their flames to the bowl, and a great swirling fire erupted from within.

The Seoul Summer Games had officially begun.

CHAPTER 7

"According to this," Nate said, his nose stuck in a *Sports Illustrated*, "Flo Jo doesn't compete until next week. So it looks like we've got some time to enjoy a bit of Seoul."

He sat on the bed, wrapped in one of the hotel's fluffy white robes that made him look like a melting marshmallow. Rachel wore another robe, sitting at the dining room table and chowing down on a giant cheeseburger. Maya had slipped down to the lobby to say good-bye to her dad, who had another full day of meetings.

"We've never really had a chance to sightsee when we time-travel," Rachel said between bites.

The elevator door opened, and Maya stepped into the penthouse.

"Nate!" Rachel hissed. "Put the magazine away, stupid."

Nate quickly hid the *Sports Illustrated* magazine in the pocket of his robe.

Maya was not her usual, bubbly self. Her shoulders were slumped, and she barely lifted her feet as she trudged across the room. She slumped into a chair next to Rachel.

Nate excused himself to get dressed in the adjoining room. He'd picked up a few novelty T-shirts and shorts at the hotel's gift shop. Maya had insisted. "Charge it to the room," she'd said coyly.

She wasn't coy now, though. And Rachel knew exactly why.

"He works a lot, doesn't he?" she asked.

Maya sighed, nodded. "All the time." She broke off a piece of bread from the loaf on the room service tray and nibbled on it. "I mean, I shouldn't complain," she said. "Look at where I am. What I get to do. How bodacious is this? Still . . . it'd be nice to sleep in my own bed. In my own home."

"Trust me," Rachel said. "I know the feeling."

Nate burst back into the room, wearing a T-shirt that said *SEOUL!* in bold letters and a pair of shorts. "All right," he said. "Who wants to be tourists?!"

Maya perked up. "I do," she said.

Rachel shook her head. "What a dork," she whispered so only Maya could hear.

The trio of teens spent the remainder of the day exploring the city. They rode the Seoul Metro train, stopping at beautiful destinations like the Changdeokgung Palace, a 600-year-old building made of wood and set on a stone platform. The palace also had sprawling gardens, tiled roofs, and intricate carvings throughout.

They spent the next few days doing more of the same, seeing sights like the National Museum of Korea and an ancient temple called the Bongeunsa Temple. Though Rachel found the sites awe-inspiring, she found Nate's tendency to spout little factoids about each place grating.

"Did you know," he said as they walked through the temple. "The temple was founded back in 794 during the reign of—"

Rachel interrupted him by making loud snoring sounds. She looked at Maya, who covered her mouth with one hand to stifle a giggle.

Through it all, Rachel found herself bonding with Maya. Each day when Mr. Gordon left for work, the same hurt expression crossed Maya's face. It was a look that Rachel knew well. And each day, Rachel did her best to make that expression disappear. She often walked side by side with her new friend while Nate shuffled along behind them.

Despite their touristy travel, the teens also paid close attention to the Games. Each night, they'd catch up on the day's events and watch from high above as throngs of people left Jamsil Stadium.

They used their all-access passes to visit the Jamsil Indoor Swimming Pool on the day that

U.S. diver Greg Louganis leaped from the board, rotated in mid-air, and struck the back of his head on the diving board before splashing into the water. The crowd gasped and grew silent as he climbed from the pool holding his head.

Thirty minutes and five stitches later, Louganis performed the best dive of the day and went on to capture gold.

They saw the U.S. women's gymnastics team penalized after an alternate appeared on the uneven bars, a mistake that landed them in fourth place while both the men's *and* women's teams from the Soviet Union won gold.

And they definitely hit Jamsil Stadium to see some of the athletic events, including Flo Jo's qualifying and quarter-final heats in the 100-meter dash. She looked solid in each race and was easily the person to beat.

By the time the sun cracked over the horizon on the day of Florence Joyner's gold medal 100-meter race, Nate and Rachel had taken full advantage of the all-access passes, seeing the Olympics like they'd never seen them before.

The excitement in the arena was electric.

Rachel fidgeted with the lanyard around her neck as she, Maya, and Nate entered the arena. Even though she knew history would repeat itself—that Flo Jo would take home her first gold medal—she still, somehow, was nervous.

Rachel was once more dressed in one of Maya's colorful outfits. They were clothes she'd never even consider wearing at home, but with Maya it felt all right to stand out. Her companion wore a patriotic red-, white-, and blue-striped shirt plastered with stars. Nate followed along. Their seats were even better than the ones they'd had for the Opening Ceremonies. They were so close to the track infield, Rachel could see the beads of sweat on the athletes' foreheads, could hear their ragged breathing after a race.

A series of semi-final races occurred first. When Florence Joyner's name was called over the speakers, Rachel craned her neck to peer out at the starting line. "Where is Flo Jo?" she asked.

Maya pointed. "There," she said.

Unlike the Olympic time trials, Joyner did not stand out from the rest of the competitors. No flashy leotard. No sparkles or leggings. Just a simple red-and-white uniform, same as the other U.S. athletes.

She won her semi-final race with the remarkable time of 10.7 seconds.

There was a brief pause after the semi-finals were complete. Rachel watched Flo Jo keenly as she spoke with Al Joyner. He appeared to have shut off all of his husband emotions and was focused on simply being her coach.

At last, the time for the gold medal race arrived.

"One hundred meters, final," the voice on the loudspeaker said. "Racers take your mark."

Flo Jo stood before lane three while her U.S. teammate, Evelyn Ashford, was in lane six.

Maya cupped her hands around her mouth. "Come on, Flo Jo!" she shouted.

Joyner took a last breath and placed her feet into the blocks. Rachel tensed up as if she were also gearing up for a race. Both of Flo Jo's hands were on the track, and her head faced down. Her curly black hair spilled over her shoulders and hid her face.

Keep your head down! Rachel heard Coach Hartford's voice echo in her mind.

Flo Jo looked up, and the wind brushed the hair away. From their spot in the crowd, Rachel could see the determination on the athlete's face.

The biggest stage in the world.

All eyes on Flo Jo.

Bang!

The sprinters tore out of the blocks, coming up fast. Time seemed to slow as Rachel leaned forward to watch. Maya reached over and took Rachel's hand, gripping it tightly as they watched.

Joyner's strides were fluid, precise. She didn't bounce around, didn't have any extra bit of movement that would slow her down. She simply glided along the track like her feet were barely touching it.

Just over halfway through the race, Flo Jo broke out into a giant grin. The gold was hers, and she knew it.

As she crossed the finish line and fell to a heap on the track, Maya leapt from her seat. "She did it!" she shouted, grabbing Rachel and pulling her up, as well. "Ten-point-five-four seconds! That's radical!"

CHAPTER 8

Maya swept Rachel into a hug. The two cheered and laughed, two peas in a pod. After Maya set her back down, a smiling Rachel glanced over at Nate. He was still in his seat, watching not the track, but the two girls beside him.

"Flo Jo just won gold," she said. "Why are you acting like a buzzkill?"

Nate stood. "I . . . I think I'm gonna go back to the hotel," he said. "I'm not feeling well."

Rachel was confused. "Why?"

Maya appeared over Rachel's shoulder. "Come on, Rach," she said. "I see some people with passes going down onto the infield. I think we can join them."

Rachel spied Al Joyner on the track, a huge U.S. flag on a pole in his hands. He waved it joyously in the air.

"Let's go," Maya said. She couldn't wait any longer. The brightly-clad teen headed into the crowd, down the cement steps, and toward the track's infield.

"Maya! Wait up!" Rachel yelled. She grabbed Nate's wrist. "Hurry up, slowpoke. Move those turkey legs or we're gonna lose her."

Nate didn't budge. He jerked his arm out of her grip. "Knock it off," he said.

"Knock *what* off?" Rachel asked. "Nate, we don't have time for your childish pouting."

"Whatever." He shrugged off the backpack and dropped it to the ground. "I can't believe you're acting so shallow, like you don't even see how you're treating me. Like I'm a . . . *a joke*. . . while you and Maya pretend you're BFFs."

"A joke?"

"Enjoy acting like Aly Wainwright and spending time with your new, rich friend." Nate turned on a heel and started to storm off.

"Nate!" she called after him.

"Rachel! Come on!" Maya had stopped and was waving her forward. Nate was still in sight but was headed back toward the stadium entrance.

"I see Flo Jo!" Maya hollered. Rachel spun her head, and Maya was jumping up and down, pointing to her left.

What do I do? What do I do?

Rachel looked back. Nate was gone.

He'll be all right, she tried to convince herself. *He knows how to get back to the hotel. He just needs some time to cool off.*

Rachel began to weave through the crowd toward Maya. Suddenly she stopped. "Oh! Almost forgot." She hurried back and plucked the backpack containing the magical *Sports Illustrated* magazines off the ground.

The crowd began to swell, like the current of the ocean, and Rachel only saw flickers of her friend. "Maya!" She tried to get the girl's attention but failed.

A woman in a red and white leotard breezed past, and Rachel was almost certain it was Evelyn Ashford, who'd finished in second place.

"Maya!"

The flickers of color were gone. Maya was lost in the crowd, and Rachel had to fend for herself.

She elbowed her way forward until she was down on the infield. Rachel clutched the straps of the backpack tightly. She looked left, then right. Maya was nowhere to be seen.

"Oof!" Rachel was not looking when she collided with another person. The backpack fell out of her hands. Rachel turned, began to say, "I'm sorry," and stopped after the *I'm*.

The person she'd run into was Florence Griffith Joyner.

"It's all right," Joyner said with a smile.

The gold medal athlete was more striking up close. Her face and body were angular and fit. She had beautiful, piercing eyes, and her long, flowing hair framed her face.

Rachel struggled to say something. *What do you say to one of the most influential female athletes in American history?*

She finally found a phrase, saying, "Congratulations on your gold medal."

"Thanks," Joyner said.

"You're, well, you're a really big inspiration to a lot of people," Rachel said. "And you will be for a very long time."

"Why, that means a lot," Joyner said. "You know, people used to tease me at school. For my hair and my clothes. So I started dressing unique, making people look at me a different way. Because being confident about who you are will make you a winner every time."

Suddenly, the hair on the back of Rachel's neck began to rise. The air around her grew warm and crackled. Joyner did not seem to notice; she was waving at someone behind Rachel.

Rachel looked down at the pack in her hands. Even though it was zipped tight, she could see the flicker of blue energy from within.

Oh, no! she thought. *What about Nate?!*

He was back at the hotel, or on his way. Nowhere near the magazines.

If he's not with me, he won't be able to jump back home.

Rachel looked up at the 100-meter champion. "Uh . . . " she stammered. "Excuse me."

"Sure thing." Around them, people began to chant Flo Jo's name. She extended a hand and waved to them.

For a brief moment, Rachel wondered where Maya had disappeared to. It didn't matter, though. Because she couldn't take Maya with her. She had to reach Nate before it was too late.

Rachel jostled her way through the crowd, throwing elbows as she went. One older man cursed at her as she struck him in the stomach. She didn't even have time to holler an apology. She broke free of the crowd and sprinted along the edge of the track. The backpack crackled and glowed, and she could feel the world begin to spin.

There's no time!

She urged herself forward. Off the track. Up the stadium stairs. Out the door. Back onto the streets of Seoul.

Ahead of her, the Grand Seoul Hotel stood like a glittering beacon in the glinting sunlight.

"Nate!" she nearly screamed at the top of her lungs.

He wasn't there.

She wasn't going to make it back.

It was too late.

Three brilliant flashes of light erupted, and in an instant, everything went black.

CHAPTER 9

The music was back.

The darkness of Grandpa Sam's basement returned.

The ceiling thumped to the beat of a song Rachel couldn't recognize. It had been over a week since she and Nate had vanished from the cabin. She wasn't entirely sure, but Rachel thought it was the same song that had been playing when they'd left.

She rose to her feet as her clouded mind suddenly cleared. Her fight with Nate. His storming off. Her being without him when the magazine sparked and guided her back.

Panic dropped like a heavy blanket on her shoulders. "Nate?!"

What if he didn't make it back? What if he's trapped in 1988?

"Nate!"

Rachel found the light switch and clicked it
on. Shadows fled as the light illuminated Grandpa
Sam's memorabilia collection.

She searched the basement. Nate was
nowhere to be found.

The song above ended, leaving Rachel in eerie
silence. Then, from the living room, she heard
Jerrika's voice. "Did you guys see that? It was
a flash of light or something. Is someone taking
pictures outside?"

Rachel took the basement steps two at a time.
She nearly sprinted into the crowded living room.
She would have cared more about the mess in
Grandpa Sam's cabin if Nate wasn't in danger.

"Hey Rachel," Aly Wainwright said. She sat
on the kitchen island, swinging her legs, carefree.
"What happened to your dorky cousin?"

"You mean Nate?" Rachel said, glaring as
she hurried past Aly and weaved through a few
others until she reached the living room.

Jerrika stood by the window, peering out into the black. "I think someone's out there," she said. "Again. This party is weirding me out."

Rachel tried to see out the window but couldn't, so she ran to the door and out into the night. She sprinted along the side of the cabin to the trees and the lake's shoreline.

By the faint blue moonlight, she saw a figure lying in the grass.

"Nate! Nate, is that you?"

He coughed and sat up as she called his name. One last crackle of blue energy flitted from around him. "Rachel?" He sounded confused. "Why am I . . . outside?"

Rachel hurried over, skidding to her knees in front of him. She wrapped him up in a big hug. "I was so worried," she said. "But you're here. You're okay."

"We . . . we jumped back," he said. "But not together."

"How?"

Nate reached for the back pocket of his jeans. From it, he withdrew a rolled-up, bent issue of *Sports Illustrated*. The one from the Indianapolis time trials.

"You had it with you?" Rachel asked.

Nate nodded. "I was mad at you," he said. "But I'm not insane."

Rachel hugged him tighter. "I'm so sorry I acted like a jerk to you."

"It's okay," Nate said, his voice squeaking out.

"You're not a joke," she continued. "I shouldn't have treated you like one."

They stood. Rachel brushed pine needles and grass clippings from Nate's shirt. Together they walked back into the cabin.

"What is going on?" Aly asked as they entered the kitchen again. Her face was scrunched up, her nose upturned. "I'm getting, like, total deja vu."

"I think everyone should leave," Rachel announced, walking to Grandpa Sam's record player and clicking it off.

"Are you feeling okay?" Aly asked.

Rachel thought about it. She shook her head. "No," she said. "I'm not." But it wasn't sickness she felt. She was ashamed she'd broken her grandpa's trust by coming there, all so that she could fit in and be cool.

Aly shrugged. "Whatever," she said.

Slowly, the group of teenagers in Grandpa Sam's cabin filtered out until only Nate and Rachel remained. Nate and Rachel *and* a big mess.

They spent the next hour cleaning. Nate collected the scattered garbage while Rachel vacuumed.

As they straightened the living room, Nate stopped and said, "Rachel. Check it out." He was standing in front of the gigantic bookshelf, pointing at a book.

Rachel walked over as he pulled the hardcover book off the shelf. He handed it to her.

Florence Joyner was on the cover, mid-stride and smiling. The photo had been taken as she crossed the finish line after winning gold in the 100-meter dash.

"*Speed and Style*," Rachel said, reading the book's title. "*The Life of Florence Griffith Joyner*. By—"

She stopped there because she couldn't believe the author's name. "By Maya Gordon," she said, finally recovering.

The book had been published recently. Rachel turned it over. The author photo on the dust jacket was Maya, all right. She was in her late thirties now, wearing a glittering gold top and sunglasses. But the smile and her style hadn't changed a bit.

"Maya wrote a biography of Flo Jo," Nate said.

"Tubular," Rachel said.

She took the book to her room and placed it on the futon bed to read later.

When the cabin looked the same as it had when she'd arrived hours—*days!*—earlier, Rachel and Nate walked to the basement. There, they replaced the magazines in their rightful slots in the file cabinet. Rachel gave the key one final turn.

It softly clicked.

"Come on," she said, "Let's go."

Since they didn't have school the following day, Rachel and Nate and the Wells track and field teams spent the humid morning preparing for the final meet. It was the last push, and Coach Hartford was determined to make sure her troops were ready for battle. They ran sprints until they were all just sweaty lumps in running shoes.

Aly and the other girls were quiet around Rachel. They weren't *acting* mad at her for canceling the party early the night before, but it was hard to tell if they *were* actually upset.

That was the least of Rachel's concerns, though. She couldn't seem to focus during her 100-meter practice runs. They were clunky and forced. Oftentimes, she would forget Coach Hartford's direction when coming out of the blocks, picking her head up or reacting like a scared animal to the whistle.

After practice, a frustrated Rachel shoved her uniform into her duffel bag, met Nate outside the locker rooms, and waited for their ride home.

When Uncle Peter's car finally pulled into the lot, he had a very special guest in the passenger seat.

"Mom!" Rachel dropped her duffel bag as her mom stepped from the car.

"Hey, kiddo," her mom said as the two embraced. "Miss me?"

"You have no idea."

As they pulled into the driveway at Grandpa Sam's cabin, Rachel spied the trailer backed up to the garage. Its door hung open. As they parked, Aunt Holly stepped out of the trailer carrying a blue bin.

The rest of our things, Rachel thought. *It's really done. Mom and Dad are divorced, and my life is in Wells.* Despite the time and adventures she and Nate had been on recently, Rachel hadn't really considered not spending part of her life in Boston. With her dad. But now that the reality was in front of her, a piece of her heart ached.

They unpacked the trailer, stacking the bins and boxes in Grandpa Sam's garage. Soon, Rachel and her mom would be looking for a place of their own in Wells. An apartment. A small house. Until then, though, Rachel would gladly sleep in the cabin's makeshift bedroom.

The whole afternoon, Rachel was afraid that Grandpa Sam would find something—a missed can of soda, a stray Cheeto on the floor—that would give away her mistake from the night before. Thankfully, she and Nate had done a spectacular job cleaning up.

That night, after a family dinner made by Grandpa Sam, and after Nate and his parents had left, Rachel sat alone on the office futon. She read from Maya's book, learning more about Flo Jo than she'd known when she'd briefly met the athlete.

She learned that Flo Jo won the Jesse Owens National Youth Games when she was fourteen, just a year older than Rachel. It was weird to think that she'd actually met Owens, too, back in 1936 on their very first time-travel experience.

My life is bizarro, Rachel marveled.

She also read about Joyner's death, a sad fact she had not known. The gold medalist had died very young, at the age of 38, after suffering an epileptic seizure. Rachel read this part of the biography through tears. She could tell, from the way that Maya wrote about her hero, that Maya's passion for Flo Jo was true and enduring.

There was a soft knock on the door. Her mom poked her head in. "Got a minute?" she asked.

Rachel smiled. "Of course." She wiped her eyes and closed the book.

"You okay?" her mom asked.

"I'm just . . . nervous for tomorrow," Rachel said, which was mostly true.

Her mom came in and sat down on the thin futon mattress beside her. "Whatcha reading?"

"Oh, nothing," Rachel said. *Only a book about a woman I talked to after she won Olympic gold in the 100-meter dash written by a person who I hung out with in South Korea in 1988. No big deal.*

"Hey, I loved Flo Jo," her mom said. "I used to watch her race when I was your age." She nodded at the book. "Looking for some inspiration?"

"Something like that."

Her mom stood. "Don't worry about tomorrow," she said. "Just do the best you can, be true to yourself, and you'll do great. There's nobody else like you in the entire world, Rachel."

When she was alone again, Rachel flipped open the book once more, and saw a photograph of Flo Jo as a teenager. Even then, her sense of style and uniqueness made her stand out.

The photo gave her an idea.

She sent Nate a text, hoping it wasn't too late and that he wasn't sleeping off the adventure they'd just returned from. *U AWAKE?*

Ten seconds later: *YEP. WHAT'S UP?*

Rachel's mind was made up. She didn't even hesitate. *I NEED YOUR HELP W/ SOMETHING.*

CHAPTER 10

The final conference meet of the season took place in the city of Hollingsworth, about thirty miles from Wells, at a small community college.

Rachel had her earbuds plugged in. Loud music filled her head in an effort to calm her nerves. She sat next to Nate on the infield, where most of the Wells Warriors had gathered to stretch.

Rachel straightened her blue and yellow tracksuit jacket.

"You nervous?" Nate asked.

Rachel shrugged. "Not really," she said.

"Liar," Nate said with a smile.

They had been up late the night before, working on their "special project." Well, *Nate* had. Rachel had just paced around and made him anxious.

The rest of the Warriors also wore blue and yellow tracksuits. They huddled together while

Coach Hartford and the boys' team coach, a hulking man by the name of Coach Beckett, strategized.

The hurdles and relay races were first. Nate's 4x100-meter relay squad won their semi-final race but came up short in the final. They took third place. Nate, who ran anchor for the team, had become surprisingly agile and confident on the track. Part of that had to do with the knowledge they learned from Jesse Owens, who'd taught Nate his method of racing.

Near lunchtime, the voice on the sound system said, "Last call for girls one hundred-meter dash, semi-finals."

Aly, Shelby, and Rachel stood side by side while they waited to race. The first two runners in each heat advanced to the final.

Rachel was scheduled to race in the first heat.

"You ready?" Nate asked.

Rachel nodded.

She unzipped her track jacket and slid out of it.

The leotard underneath was unlike anything the other racers had ever seen. Sparkling sequins shone in the sun, casting a kaleidoscope of light. Blue and yellow stripes ran in zig-zags across her chest and back. As she shed her track pants, the lightning bolt continued down one leg, much like the tendrils of energy that enveloped her and Nate when they traveled in time.

Rachel heard whispers and coughs. All eyes turned to her.

Standing nearby, Aly Wainwright asked, "What in the world is *that?*"

That, Rachel thought, *is the girl who's going to beat you.*

Rachel had designed the leotard, and Nate had used his skills with a sewing machine to make it. She was very proud of their work and wore it with confidence.

"*Racers, take your mark!*"

Rachel walked to the track. The other racers in her heat stared at her.

Rachel was in lane three, in-between two sprinters from Morristown. One of the girls looked at Rachel and said, "Wicked suit."

"Thanks," Rachel said.

She stretched, bent down, and placed her feet into the starting blocks.

"Set!" A woman in white stood alongside the track, holding a starter's pistol high into the air.

Bang!

She was off. Head down. Body leaning forward. Legs pumping. Rachel kept her eyes on the track, not the finish line. Glinting in her periphery, dancing like fireflies on the track, were reflections from the sequins on her suit.

The Morristown racer in lane four kept stride with her at first, but Rachel put on a burst of speed and soared past the finish line in first place.

"Yes!" she shouted, pumping a victorious fist into the air.

As she came to a stop, Rachel glanced into the stands. Her mom and Aunt Holly jumped up and down. Uncle Peter had made a sign that read: *YOUNG IS #1!* It was nearly identical to the one Maya had made for Flo Jo back in Indianapolis.

She was about to head back to the team when she saw someone standing at the edge of the bleachers, nearly lost in the crowd.

"Dad?" Rachel said.

It was him, all right, with his dark brown hair a bit disheveled. He still had some facial hair but looked like he'd lost a couple pounds.

He's here. He's really here.

Their eyes locked, and her dad flashed a smile. Rachel smiled back, her heart suddenly pressed against her ribcage. She willed herself not to cry.

The announcer called for the next racers, and Rachel was forced to leave the track.

Aly Wainwright won her semi-final race by a wide margin. Shelby came in second in the last heat. All three Warriors were in the final heat.

Coach Hartford gave a pep-talk. "Not quite sure what's going on with the new outfit, Young,"

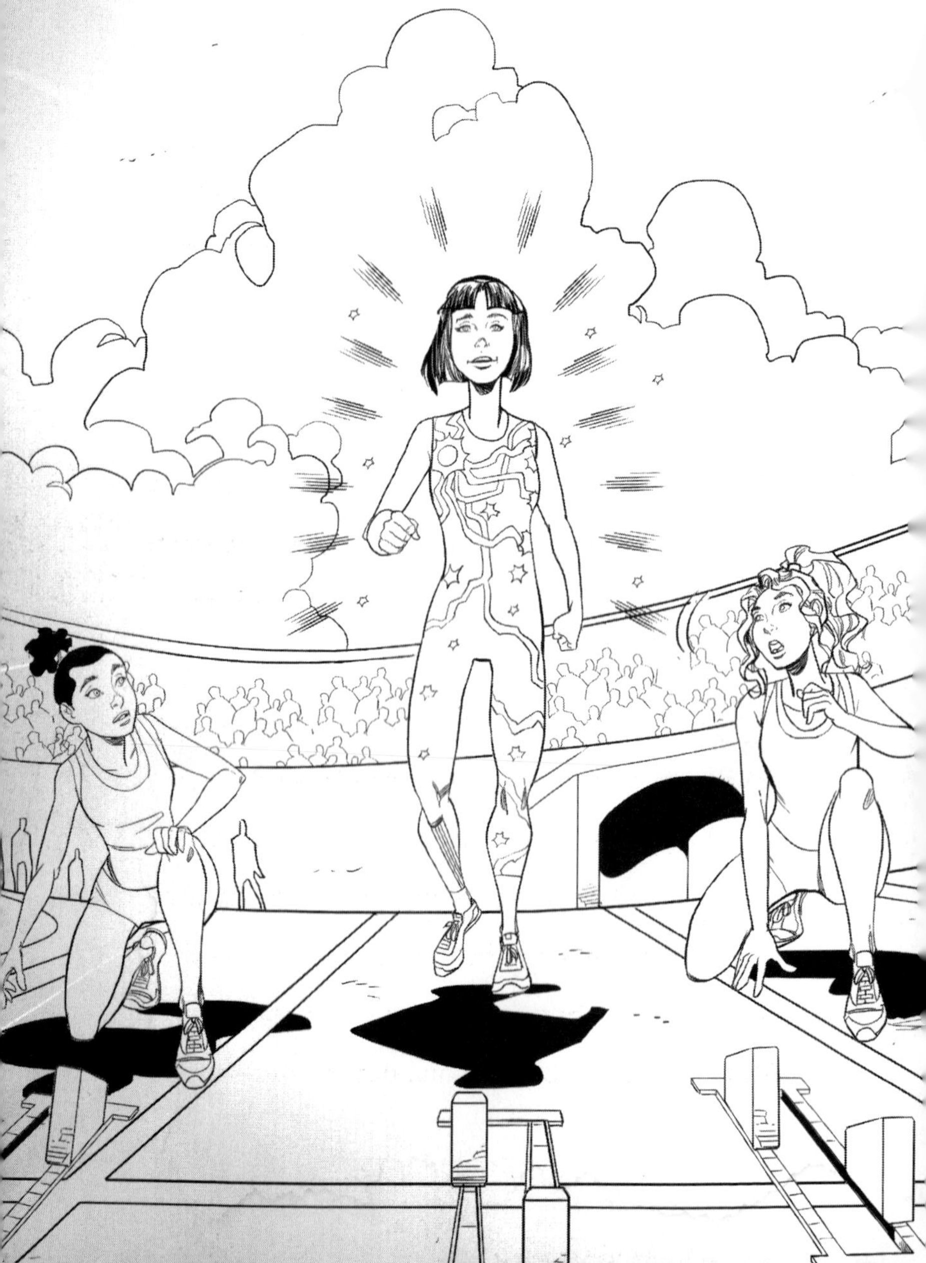

she said, "but I like it. Throws off the competition. You know who it reminds me of?"

Rachel grinned. "Yeah, I know."

The trio of Warriors walked side by side to the starting blocks. "Good luck, girls," Rachel said.

"I dig the new threads," Shelby said in her monotone. Rachel couldn't tell if she was being sarcastic, so she was just going to take it as a compliment.

"Thanks," she replied.

"Yeah," Aly said. The lilting sarcasm in her voice was easy to pinpoint. "Takes a lot of guts to come out wearing something like that." She laughed. "Good luck."

Rachel was in lane two while Aly was in lane three and Shelby was in lane one. Five other sprinters stood at the blocks with them. Each one of the girls was now in her own world, mentally preparing for the race about to be run.

Rachel found her thoughts drifting to her dad . . . to Maya . . . to the outrageous outfit she wore.

"*Racers take your mark!*"

She cast aside those memories and focused on the race. Rachel slid her foot into the block. She bent forward, her leg muscles straining as she placed her hands on the track. Her head was down, her eyes closed.

This is it.

"*Set!*"

Her every muscle quivered in anticipation as she waited for the gun. Each millisecond expanded into an infinity.

And then—

Bang!

Rachel got a clean start, swiftly surging forward. She kept her body low, her movements smooth. Next to her, Aly was a step ahead.

Always a step ahead!

Rachel's muscles screamed as she pushed harder than ever before. She wasn't going to come in second, not this time. Her powerful legs pumped like pistons, one then the other, one then the other.

Come on, come on . . .

She gained a step, and Aly was at her side. Rachel visualized the finish line but noticed a flicker of movement from the corner of her eye. Aly had turned her head *ever so briefly*, surprised that Rachel was so close.

It was the split-second difference Rachel needed.

She put on a burst of speed, digging for the last ounce of strength. The finish line was upon them. Rachel leaned forward—

—and crossed the line a half-step ahead of Aly.

I did it! I won!

The crowd erupted. Through the noise, Rachel heard her mom cheering and Grandpa Sam whistling. In fact, her whole family was jumping in sync with one another. Rachel looked to the foot of the bleachers. Her dad was still there, fists raised over his head.

Shelby, who'd come in fifth, offered her congratulations. Aly, meanwhile, stood to the side, alone. Selfish tears streaked down her face. Rachel ignored Aly and instead joined her team, who swarmed her with hugs.

Nate pointed and said to anyone in earshot, "I sewed that badboy. Not ashamed of it. I've got skills, people!"

The meet ended as the sun slipped behind the college buildings. The award ceremony was not as grand as the ones at the Olympics, but when the medal was draped over Rachel's neck, she felt like Florence Griffith Joyner.

The crowd dispersed. Rachel zipped up her tracksuit coat, covering the outrageous leotard not out of shame, but because she was actually cold. For the first time in a long while, the breeze cutting across the track infield was cool.

She and Nate walked together. A couple of girls from Morristown complimented Nate on his sewing skills. They were pretty, so of course Nate's response was to stammer and mumble.

"Smooth," Rachel said as the girls walked off.

Their family huddled together by the entrance. As they walked toward them, though, Rachel spied her dad standing alone by the bleachers.

"Go on ahead," she said to Nate.

She hadn't seen her dad in a very long time. Still, sliding into his arms and giving him a hug was the easiest thing in the world.

"Wow," he said. "I mean, wow. Great racing out there, kiddo."

"Thanks, Dad."

"I mean, it's like I always said. *She has places to go—*"

"*—and she wants to get there fast,*" Rachel finished.

Her dad grinned. "Bingo."

"Thanks for coming."

"Absolutely. No way I was gonna miss it."

"Can you stay for dinner? We'll probably go out as a team. It's kind of a tradition."

Her dad glanced over his shoulder, briefly, in the direction of her family. "Probably not. Got a long drive ahead of me." He placed a hand on her shoulder. "Tell you what, though. Next time you visit Boston, we'll hit up Mama Carla's. Deal?"

"Deal."

And together, they said, "The meatballs! *The meatballs!*"

The two laughed, and it was wonderful, and Rachel never wanted it to end. But it did, and in the lingering bit of silence, Rachel thought she'd cry.

Finally, her dad said, "I'll see you real soon, okay?"

"Okay."

"Love ya, champ."

"Love you, too."

"I'm proud of you. Great race." He shook his head in amazement and repeated, more to himself than to her, "Great race."

He backed away a few steps, like he didn't want her to leave his sight. Then he turned and made his way through the crowd.

A moment later, Rachel's mom was at her side.

"You ready?" Her mom slid an arm around her shoulder and squeezed.

Rachel watched her dad walk away, hands in his pockets, back toward the parking lot. Then she looked up at her mom and smiled away tears.

"Yeah," she said. "Let's go home."

ABOUT THE AUTHOR

Brandon Terrell is the author of numerous children's books, including several volumes in both the Tony Hawk 900 Revolutions series and the Tony Hawk Live 2 Skate series. He has also written the first four titles from the Sports Illustrated Kids Time Machine Magazine set and the latest titles in the Jim Nasium series. When not hunched over his laptop, Brandon enjoys watching movies and television, reading, watching (and playing!) baseball, and spending time with his wife and two children in Minnesota.

ABOUT THE ILLUSTRATOR

Passionate comic book fan and artist Eduardo Garcia works from his studio in Mexico City. Since signing with Space Goat Productions in 2012, he has brought his talent, pencils, and ink to such varied projects as Spider-Man Family (Marvel), Flash Gordon (Ardden), and Speed Racer (IDW).

GLOSSARY

agility – the ability to move quickly and easily.

blocks – a device used by runners, usually sprinters, for increasing their speed off the mark. It is typically made of metal or wood, secured to the ground, to brace the runner's feet

competitor – someone or something that is trying to beat or do better than others in a contest

influential – having the power to influence or to cause change

intimidate – to make timid and fill with fear

meet – a competition involving a series of athletic contests such as running and jumping, usually including track and field events

penalized – punished for breaking a rule or a law

precise – very accurate or exact

procession – a group of individuals moving along in an orderly way.

qualifying – in track and field, a specific race that is required in order to advance to the next

sprint – to race or move at full speed, often for a short distance

time trials – a test of an athlete's individual speed over a set distance where athletes are individually timed

tenacity – the quality of being very persistent and stubborn

TIMELESS FACTS:
FLORENCE GRIFFITH JOYNER

▶ Born in Los Angeles on December 21, 1959, the seventh of eleven children to Robert and Florence Griffith.

▶ Started competing in track and field at age seven and won Jesse Owens National Youth Games at age of fourteen.

▶ Followed her coach, Bob Kersee, to the University of California-Los Angeles in 1980.

▶ Won silver in the 200 meters at the 1984 L.A. Olympics.

▶ Married Olympian Al Joyner, brother of friend Jackie Joyner-Kersee.

▶ Shone brightly at 1988 Seoul Olympics with gold-medal and record-breaking dashes in 100 and 200 meters.

▶ Passed away on September 21, 1998, from epileptic siezure while sleeping at the age of 38.

TIMELESS FACTS:
THE 1988 SEOUL OLYMPICS

▶ South Korea became second Asian nation, after Japan first hosted in 1964, to host the Olympic Games.

▶ Some 8,400 athletes from 159 countries participated.

▶ Opening ceremony was the last to be featured during the daytime and included a mass demonstration of taekwondo.

▶ Tennis returned to Olympic competition for the first time since 1924; table tennis and team archery were also added.

▶ U.S. swimmer Matt Biondi was the top individual medal-winner, taking home five golds, a silver, and a bronze.

▶ Canadian sprinter Ben Jonson set the world record to win gold in the 100-meter dash but was sent home after testing positive for steroids.

▶ Canadian sailor Lawrence Lemieux, in medal-winning position at the time, abandoned his course to help save two other sailors from Singapore whose boat had capsized; for his deed, Lemieux was given the Pierre de Coubertain medal.

▶ Total of 132 medals won by the Soviet Union topped all other countries, including runners-up East Germany (102 medals) and the United States (94 medals); it also marked the last Olympic competition for the Soviet Union and East Germany.

FIND YOUR MOMENT
IN TIME WITH

SPORTS ILLUSTRATED KIDS

TIME MACHINE
MAGAZINE